Shadows Are About

by ANN WHITFORD PAUL

Illustrated by
MARK GRAHAM

SCHOLASTIC
HARDCOVER

Scholastic Inc. ◆ New York

Library of Congress Cataloging-in-Publication Data

Paul, Ann Whitford.
Shadows are about / by Ann Whitford Paul;
illustrated by Mark Graham.   p.   cm.
Summary: Shadows are alive, climbing, spinning, swooping, and
stretching with everything around them during the bright sunny day,
but when night falls . . . the shadows disappear.
ISBN 0-590-44842-0
[1. Shadows—Fiction.]   I. Graham, Mark, ill.   II. Title.
PZ7.P278338Sh   1991   91-19318
[E]—dc20   CIP
                         AC

12 11 10 9 8 7 6 5 4 3 2 1   2 3 4 5 6/9

Printed in the U.S.A.   36

First Scholastic printing, May 1992

Designed by Tracy Halliday

Mark Graham's artwork was
done in oil paint
on paper.

For my children,
Henya, Jonathon, Alan, and Sarah,
always an inspiration.
—A.W.P.

To Tyler and Jenny
—M.G.

It is day. The sun is out.

Inside, outside, shadows are about.

They drive with cars and sway with trees.

They droop with flowers and fall with leaves.

They stretch with cats and chase with dogs.

They swim with ducks and jump with frogs.

Shadows run. Shadows skip.

Sometimes shadows turn a flip.

They flap with flags . . .

. . . and swoop with kites.

They roll with hoops . . .

. . . and race with bikes.

Shadows hop. Shadows stand.
Shadows march beside a band.

Late-day shadows stretch through rooms.
They sit with chairs and lean with brooms.

Shadows climb up and down.

Shadows bounce around . . . around.

They clap with hands and roll with balls.
They paint dark pictures on the walls.

But when the day turns into night . . .

. . . shadows *never* stay . . . without a light.